THE
NIGHT BEFORE
CHRISTMAS
IN ARIZONA

Sue Carabine

Illustrations by
Shauna Mooney Kawasaki

Gibbs Smith, Publisher

First Edition
06 05 04 03 02   5 4 3 2 1

Text and illustrations © 2002 by Gibbs Smith, Publisher

All rights reserved. No part of this book may be reproduced
by any means whatsoever without written permission from
the publisher, except brief portions quoted for the purpose
of review.

Published by
Gibbs Smith, Publisher
P.O. Box 667
Layton, Utah 84041

Orders: (1-800) 748-5439
www.gibbs-smith.com

Designed and produced by
    Mary Ellen Thompson, TTA Designs
Printed in China

ISBN 1-58685-169-1
ISBN 1-58685-221-3 gift

'Twas the night before Christmas;
the reindeer and Nick
Were flying down low
over Route 66.

They felt a warm breeze,
smelled a citrus aroma,
And arrived at their most
favorite state—Arizona!

St. Nick and his deer loved
this state, east to west,
And wherever they went,
they were treated as guests.

Over Monument Valley
and Glen Canyon Dam,
Santa cried, "I'm so glad
to be back here, I am!

"The 'snowbirds' who come here
just don't want to leave;
They love to spend Christmas
in air they can breathe!"

He mused at Grand Canyon
as they made that HUGE leap:
"Remember when this, boys,
was a hundred feet deep?

"And, can you believe it?
It seems just yesterday
When this hole in the ground
would scare no one away."

Nick's kind face then changed,
for a moment looked sad,
"Am I getting too old
to do Christmas, my lads?

"I thought as we flew
over balmy Sun City,
The folks who live there
have no need of our pity

" 'Cause mostly they're seniors,
content as can be;
I'll bet they would welcome
an old guy like me.

"I'll give it some thought
over this Christmas season,
And ask Mrs. Claus
if she sees a reason

"Why someone else younger
should perhaps take my place.
I'll know how she feels
by the look on her face.

"Now, Dasher and Dancer,
how fast can you go?
The kids down in Phoenix
expect a great show!

"They've gathered together
at a ballpark called BOB;
If I don't get there soon,
we might bungle this job!"

It took just a jiffy,
a leap and a bound,
The deer gently landed
the sleigh on the mound.

Said Nick, "Johnson, Schilling—
you're simply the best!
Your D-Backs beat Yankees—
now, who would have guessed?!"

Just then a small boy
jumped right up on his knee,
"Dear Santa," he cried,
"please do something for me."

"Chad, how may I help you?"
Nick softly replied.
"It's Tiffany, my sister—
her puppy dog died!

"She says there's no Santa;
she says it's not true!
There's no one can help her, Nick,
no one but you."

So Nick flew to Tucson,
I-10 through Tempe,
Left a cute pup for Tiffany
under the tree.

Then next on to Yuma

to answer a letter

From a sweet girl named Chelsea

who longed to feel better.

She'd come down with measles,

had requested a book—

That one about lost boys

and a captain named Hook!

Nick smiled. *Peter Pan*
was a favorite of his,
And he knew he had something
in common with kids,

Especially the kind
who would never grow old.
"Just like me!" he cried,
watching a sunset of gold.

Nick checked out his list
high atop Humphrey's Peak,
Found the Hunts, a nice couple
he'd heard of last week.

They lived there in Flagstaff,
their kids were all grown,
Said they didn't need Christmas
now they were alone.

So Santa dropped by to
proclaim the good news:
"Your grandkids will visit
from Lake Havasu!"

Well, the Hunts didn't know
the kids' parents had planned
Another vacation—
till Nick took a hand.

The children had written,
"Nick, Mom and Dad said,
'We'll catch Grandma and Grandpa
at Easter instead.

" 'It's so much more fun
seeing Old London Bridge.'
But, Nick, we protested!"
You see, Joshua and Midge

Both yearned to spend Christmas
with Nana and Pop,
Who, in turn, were so joyful,
their smiles wouldn't stop!

It had been quite a while
since they'd seen those dear kids,
So the Hunts were just thrilled
with what Santa Claus did.

They welcomed Nick's presence
with a great deal of fuss.
"We know that you bring joy
to folks just like us.

"We'll never again
let this season go by
And not think of you, Nick.
You're such a great guy!"

Next, Santa Claus stopped
to see Matthew, a child
Who had one Christmas wish—
to see life in the wild.

They flew off together
o'er water and land
To awesome Lake Powell
and Painted Desert sand.

At Petrified Forest
they paused for a rest;
Sunset Crater Volcano
was one of the best!

With calm desert tortoises,
fearless black bears,
Tarantulas, coyotes—
Matt loved being there!

"You granted my wish, Nick!"
Matt cried, home again.
"I'm so grateful you showed me
the place I live in."

Near a ghost town named Christmas,
Nick hoped to assist
Still one more small family
who topped his long list.

Rob Taylor, their dad,
had to travel statewide
In his job as a salesman;
he worried inside

That he wouldn't be home
for the Yuletide this year;
He was sad and so homesick—
he needed some cheer!

At NAU, U of A,
then ASU,
Rob finished his work
and was now traveling to

Mesa and Scottsdale
and other large towns,
When he smelled spicy goodies,
heard holiday sounds.

Well! Santa swept through,
packed Rob snug on his sled,
And took off for Christmas
'fore the kids went to bed.

"Dad's home!" cried the Taylors.
Rob solemnly vowed,
"Each Yuletide I'll be here—
they make me so proud!"

He hugged his young family,
then thought, "I'll remember
The love of our family,
the joys of December!"

As Nick waved farewell,
he felt so good inside
Just knowing he'd helped
Arizonans statewide;

And he had made sure
all "his kids" shed no tear.
No, he wasn't too old
to do Christmas each year!

At last he called softly,
"Lads, time to take flight.
Merry Christmas, Arizona,
To all a good night!"